CARL GOES SHOPPING

Alexandra Day

CARL GOES SHOPPING

Farrar Straus Giroux · New York

For Madeleine

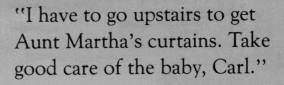

"I have to go upstairs to get Aunt Martha's curtains. Take good care of the baby, Carl."

ELECTRONICS

VISIT OUR NEW PET ARTMENT
th Floor

New!
K-9 DIVINE
SLEEPING
PILLOWS

"Good dog, Carl!"